Samuel French Acting Edition

The Keen Collection
One-Acts by Contemporary Playwrights
Volume 4

How The Moon Would Talk
by Nick Gandiello

Landlines
by Hannah Bos & Paul Thureen

30 Million
Music & Lyrics by Max Vernon
Book by Jason Kim

SAMUELFRENCH.COM   SAMUELFRENCH.CO.UK

FOR PRODUCTION ENQUIRIES

UNITED STATES AND CANADA
Info@SamuelFrench.com
1-866-598-8449

UNITED KINGDOM AND EUROPE
Plays@SamuelFrench.co.uk
020-7255-4302

Each title is subject to availability from Samuel French, depending upon country of performance. Please be aware that *THE KEEN COLLECTION: VOLUME 4* may not be licensed by Samuel French in your territory. Professional and amateur producers should contact the nearest Samuel French office or licensing partner to verify availability.

be invented, including mechanical, electronic, photocopying, recording, videotaping, or otherwise, without the prior written permission of the publisher. No one shall upload this title(s), or part of this title(s), to any social media websites.

For all enquiries regarding motion picture, television, and other media rights, please contact Samuel French.

MUSIC USE NOTE

Licensees are solely responsible for obtaining formal written permission from copyright owners to use copyrighted music in the performance of this play and are strongly cautioned to do so. If no such permission is obtained by the licensee, then the licensee must use only original music that the licensee owns and controls. Licensees are solely responsible and liable for all music clearances and shall indemnify the copyright owners of the play(s) and their licensing agent, Samuel French, against any costs, expenses, losses and liabilities arising from the use of music by licensees. Please contact the appropriate music licensing authority in your territory for the rights to any incidental music.

IMPORTANT BILLING AND CREDIT REQUIREMENTS

If you have obtained performance rights to this title, please refer to your licensing agreement for important billing and credit requirements.

TABLE OF CONTENTS

ABOUT KEEN TEENS

Keen Company is an award-winning Off Broadway theatre dedicated to wholehearted storytelling, now in its seventeenth Season. The cornerstone of the company's outreach and educational efforts is Keen Teens. The program improves the quality of plays written for high school students by commissioning scripts from accomplished New York City playwrights. This free program for students provides invaluable mentorship opportunities – working alongside professional writers, directors, and designers to rehearse and premiere new work.

When first creating Keen Teens, which is now in its eleventh year, the company found that teachers did not have access to material that was intended for a high school stage. Educators were left with either presenting classic plays never designed for teen actors, or producing simple skits that lacked rich material relevant to modern students. Central to Keen Company's mission is to produce theatre that patrons can identify with and connect to, however no such material existed for students and educators. Keen Teens brings the company's values to the high school stage by developing new work tailored specifically to be relevant and engaging to teen actors and audiences.

Keen Teens commissions and presents work that speaks to teens on their level, creating work that is as complex and multilayered as the high school world. Form, style, and context varies amongst each playwright and season. Topics have included cyberbullying and teen suicide (*Why Aren't You Dead Already?* by Halley Feiffer), same-sex relationships amongst athletes (*Going Left* by Kristoffer Diaz), environmental concerns (*A Polar Bear in New Jersey* by Anna Moench), and death within a family (*Syd Arthur* by Kenny Finkle). All pieces deal honestly and provocatively with their subject matter – some through comedy and farce, some through sincerity and intimate portraits.

As well as being tailored to the social and emotional world of teens, each piece is also designed to be accessible to educators and drama festivals. Commissions consist of thirty-minute plays, simple designs, large casts, and flexible genders. These requirements are designed so that high schools might include as many students as possible and present their productions on their own, in an evening, or as part of a competition.

Every year the Keen Teens program culminates in the world premiere performances of three newly commissioned one-act plays at The Lion Theatre in Theater Row, New York City. Since 2005, Keen Teens has made possible the Off Broadway debut of over three hundred young actors and has led to the publication of over twenty-five new one-act plays. Not only are these plays regularly produced in the United States, but in various countries around the world from Australia to Singapore.

For more information, please visit *www.keencompany.org/teens*.

KEEN TEENS ANGELS

42nd Street Development Corporation, Lindsay Adkins, Joanne Ainsworth, Sarah Alexander, Cathy and Robert Altholz, Howard Balaban, Amy and Brad Ball, Jeffrey Blair and Ivor Clark, Jeffery and Tina Bolton, Bill and Casey Bradford, Blake and Josh Bradford, Kathleen Chalfant, Buena Chilstrom, Gary and Ellen Cohen, Michael Coratolo, Elizabeth Corradino, Rose Courtney, Alexander Coxe, Katherine Crost, Michela Daliana, Lucy and Nat Day, Joseph Deasy, Mia Dillon and Keir Dullea, Emily Donahoe, Linda D'Onofrio, Maralène Downs, Mary Durante, David Ehrich and Chris Shyer, Rhonda Paul and Mark A. Feldman, Patricia Follert, Jack and Ann Gilpin, Timothy Grandia, Benjamin Goldberg, Sylvia Golden, Barbara McIntyre Hack, Richard and Edith Hanley, Erin Hogan, Sally and Robert Huxley, Stephen Kantor, David and Kate Kies, Jae Kim, Judith S. Lidsky, Kevin and Jana Maher, Marsha Mason, David McMahon, Andrew Miltenberg, Cynthia and Bruce Miltenberg, Nancy Morgan, Joy Pak, Merrill and Martin Pavane, David and Faith Pedowitz, Susan Shapiro and Bob Piller, Rhonda Pohl, Angela Reed and Todd Cerveris, Rebecca Randall, Diana Roitman, Nanny Lee Russell, Betsy and Norman Samet, Vincent Smith and Alice Silkworth, Jim Spare, Pat Stockhausen and Mike Emmerman, Ron Schwartz, Pamela Thomas, Louis Viel, Les Waters, Louly and Bill Williams, Alban Wilson, Marie and Alan Wolpert, Ernest and Judith Wong,

HOW THE MOON WOULD TALK

Nick Gandiello

HOW THE MOON WOULD TALK was first presented by Keen Company (Jonathan Silverstein, Artistic Director; Mark Armstrong, Director of New Work) and Samuel French, Inc. as part of the 2016 Keen Teens Festival of New Work from May 13 - 15. The performance was directed by Sash Bischoff. The cast was as follows:

ALLY . . . . Carolyn Gutierrez

DWAYNE . . . . .Edison Ventura Diaz

SMITHY. . . . . .Craig Steeley Jr.

SEJAL. . . . . Chris Rosas

ONNESHA. . . . . Favour Unigwe

TAMMY . . . . Roza Chervisnky

JENNY. . . . . .Emerson Thomas-Gregory

KATHERINE . . . . Francesca Iannacone

SAM. . . . . Maeve Farrell

CHARACTERS

All of these characters can be of any ethnicity, and the cast should
reflect the diversity of New York City.

ALLY, 17
DWAYNE, 17

SMITHY, 18
SEJAL, 16
ONNESHA, 17

TAMMY, 18
JENNY, 18
KATHERINE, 17
SAM, 16

AUTHOR'S NOTES

Slashes indicate overlap. Absent punctuation is intentional; if the
speaker's next line seems to be the beginning of a new thought, then
the absent punctuation suggests a suspended, cut off, or lost thought/
action. Lower-cases at the beginning of lines indicate that the speaker is
continuing the thought from their previous line.

1.

*(**DWAYNE** and **ALLY**, on a Harlem rooftop, observing the moon. **ALLY** agitated, **DWAYNE** subdued.)*

ALLY. I don't understand, what's a blood moon?

DWAYNE. It's not like there's literally blood on the moon.

ALLY. Did I say I thought there was literally blood on the moon?

DWAYNE. It's not like the moon is bleeding blood into the cosmos.

ALLY. Did I say some shit about the moon having a biological process or did I ask you what a / blood moon is, Dwayne?

DWAYNE. A blood moon is when like – A blood moon, Ally – is when, like, atmospherically…some shit about the atmosphere / and the colors,

ALLY. Oh great, oh good.

DWAYNE. like it looks red, and here you go.

ALLY. You got me standing on the roof of your building,

DWAYNE. Here you go, like

ALLY. when you know the cops don't want us on the roof,

DWAYNE. like instigating me.

ALLY. and you can't even clearly define for me what we're looking at. And it doesn't even look red. And I don't instigate.

(A couple breaths.)

DWAYNE. It's not 'til next week.

ALLY. What's not 'til next week?

DWAYNE. The – the thing, the –

ALLY. The atmospheric color thing you don't even know about is not 'til next week?

DWAYNE. It's not 'til the twenty-seventh, but I wanna take pictures every night.

ALLY. You wanna take pictures of the moon.

DWAYNE. Every night, leading up to it, yeah.

ALLY. Why you got me on the roof with you so you can take pictures of a thing you / don't even know about?

DWAYNE. Because the twenty-seventh is our One Year, and that just so happens to be when there's gonna be a supermoon bloodmoon thing, and I wanted to be romantic on some shit and take pictures of it every night leading it up to it then be like, "Happy anniversary, look at the supermoon blood moon," but you won't let me be romantic on some shit cuz you gotta instigate.

> (**DWAYNE** *takes out his cellphone, aims it at the moon, and snaps pictures.* **ALLY** *smiles, despite herself.*)

ALLY. You can be romantic on some shit.

DWAYNE. I wish I coulda been a naturalist yo.

ALLY. You can be a naturalist.

DWAYNE. When there were things you could still find out in the world.

Like I woulda been the dude that was like, "Yo why are there tides?" Then I woulda fucked around and figured out there's tides because the moon.

I woulda been the dude that was like why do people get old?

ALLY. Why do people what?

DWAYNE. Why do people get elderly, like where does the elderly come from in the body?

But I guess I gotta dead all that.

ALLY. There are still things to find out in the world.

DWAYNE. Like what?

(**ALLY** *is stumped. A few breaths as they observe the moon.*)

ALLY. Dwayne I don't think I instigate, okay, I just think

DWAYNE. You really do though.

ALLY. that sometimes you – can I finish a sentence though, damn. I just think that sometimes you get these plans in your head and you don't really fill me in on them

DWAYNE. You get abrasive yo.

ALLY. and then you get all attached to the plans that I don't know about. I get abrasive?

DWAYNE. You get hostile yo. And it's fine if it's like we're having a real fight,

ALLY. I can't even deal with you right now.

DWAYNE. like if we're fighting about something worth fighting about, like passionately, that's different. And if we really in this forever, like if we really one soul, like if we really gonna make a family one day outta one soul,

ALLY. How you making accusations right now?

DWAYNE. then I can't have the hostility, I can't.

ALLY. It is not hostility, it's like, it's like resentment maybe, like resentment because I was trying to tell you about my speech,

DWAYNE. No.

ALLY. I was trying to tell you I'm worried about my speech,

DWAYNE. No, that's not what you said.

ALLY. that I have anxiety about my speech about Gemma.

DWAYNE. That's not what you said. You said you weren't gonna do it.

ALLY. And you were supposed to interpret that, Dwayne, you were supposed to interpret that as me having anxiety about doing my speech tomorrow. Then you got all moody.

DWAYNE. Moody?

ALLY. You got all emo and moody and quiet, like you're the one who gets to be sad right now, and you said let's go on the roof.

DWAYNE. I thought it would be like, be like

ALLY. Romantic on some shit?

DWAYNE. Comforting. I thought it would be like comforting.

ALLY. Well it's not. Because it's about you. And right now has to be about me, I'm sorry but it does. Because I don't know what I'm gonna say about Gemma tomorrow.

What am I gonna say?

(A breath or two.)

DWAYNE. I know you're the one who gets to be sad right now.

ALLY. I was asking for real.

DWAYNE. Asking what?

ALLY. What do I say about my sister tomorrow?

*(**DWAYNE** blinks, mouth hanging open a little.)*

DWAYNE. See, this is how you, how you like

ALLY. How are you getting mad right now?

DWAYNE. corner me, you put me in a corner,

ALLY. I'm asking you advice.

DWAYNE. and I lose either way because nothing I say can be good enough. And if I say nothing then I'm insensitive, so I can't win, and you know what, you know what,

ALLY. I was asking you / to help.

DWAYNE. you're not sad, you're tryna win a fight. You don't know how to be sad, you only know how to be angry.

*(**ALLY** takes in the hurt for a moment, then steeles herself. **DWAYNE** knows how badly he has misstepped.)*

Fuck, my bad yo, I'm sorry yo.

ALLY. Aight, what I'mma do,

DWAYNE. It's affecting me too. / I'm feeling it too.

ALLY. nah, what I'mma do is leave you here on the roof so you and the moon can Snapchat or whatever, and I'mma go home to my Mom and my Dad,

DWAYNE. Please don't.

ALLY. who I left alone right now,

DWAYNE. They told you to get out the apartment, get some air!

ALLY. who I left alone right now, Dwayne, to come chill with your moody emo naturalist ass.

I guess I'll see you at the wake or whatever cuz I don't think I can talk to you for a minute.

DWAYNE. I'm hurting too.

ALLY. And I can't believe you said that thing about people getting old.

DWAYNE. What?

ALLY. About people getting elderly. Can't believe you said that.

DWAYNE. Why?

ALLY. Think about it Dwayne.

> (**DWAYNE** *understands. His regret and apology show all through is body.* **ALLY** *leaves the roof.* **DWAYNE** *glances up toward the moon briefly, angrily, then away.*)

2.

(Wind through the trees, and cars sighing and whispering along the avenues – they bring us to: Late afternoon. **SMITHY** *saunters out onto the roof, discretely carrying some shopping bags with bottles and red party cups in them.* **SEJAL** *bounces in after him. Both are in formal clothes.)*

SEJAL. Nah but I tried to tell Ms. Johnson, I tried to tell her: I already know about the birth canal.

SMITHY. True.

SEJAL. Cuz my mom raised me proper, feel me? She sat me down when I was like seven, she said look little man I'mma school you on the miracle of conception,

SMITHY. True.

SEJAL. on the responsibility of child bearing,

SMITHY. Word.

SEJAL. on the pains of labor, feel me? So why I gotta watch some dumbass "Miracle of Life" video?! I said, "Yo Ms. Johnson, I'm out, I ain't wasting my time on that video!"

And now I got detention yo, and everybody's spreading rumors about me.

SMITHY. Yo Sejal yo, it's cool that you were scared.

SEJAL. Scared?

SMITHY. You ain't gotta front, you were scared of the video.

SEJAL. See that's what everybody sayin, but I'm saying I already knew all that stuff! That's why I walked out, Smithy, cuz I been knew that stuff!

SMITHY. Aight yo.

ONNESHA. What you do, you used the coupon?

DWAYNE. Yeah the one from the magazine.

SEJAL. Oh there they go.

*(***DWAYNE*** and ***ONNESHA*** come out on the roof. ***DWAYNE*** is putting a tie on over a dress shirt – ***ONNESHA*** already in formal wear.)*

ONNESHA. You went to the Express store down on Fifth?

DWAYNE. Yeah I gotta look right, you know?

ONNESHA. You gotta knot it properly though.

SEJAL. I tied my tie right.

ONNESHA. See, me, I don't do all black you know?

SEJAL. I tied a windsor knot.

DWAYNE. *(To* **ONNESHA.***)* Nah, you don't have to.

ONNESHA. I think like a wake is like a celebration of life, you know?

SEJAL. I tied a windsor knot like the guy on YouTube did.

ONNESHA. Like I don't wanna walk in there looking like the grim reaper and everything.

SEJAL. Didn't take me that many tries or nothing, / I tied it right.

ONNESHA. Yeah, okay Sejal, we can see you tied your tie, damn!

SMITHY. Yall talk too much yo.

ONNESHA. …Wow you're so friendly, Smithy.

SMITHY. My dude about to have an emotional day yo, be respectful yo, we came up here to pay respects.

> (**SMITHY** *discreetly begins arranging the party cups in a row. The others nervously glance at* **DWAYNE,** *who just fumbles with his tie. A few breaths.)*

ONNESHA. "…Where beauty softens your grief." *(Off their looks.)* That's the slogan at the funeral home.

SEJAL. How do you soften grief? Can grief be softened?

ONNESHA. It's poetic, Sejal, damn.

SEJAL. I'm just saying like grammatically, like what does that even mean? Is that what's supposed to happen at a wake? Grief gets softened?

ONNESHA. Yes!

SMITHY. Yo Dwayne you good?

DWAYNE. Yeah I'm good.

SMITHY. You and Ally good?

DWAYNE. Oh, yeah, yeah of course yeah.

SMITHY. Good, that's good.

DWAYNE. I mean I gotta stand by her side right now.

SMITHY. Hell yeah.

DWAYNE. Cuz when you committed like we committed, you gotta be there for this kinda stuff.

SMITHY. Word.

DWAYNE. Like one day when we married,

ONNESHA. Married?

DWAYNE. we gonna look back on this, and it's gonna be like, be like foundational, you know? Like part of our foundation as a couple. And, and when we have kids, we'll tell them this story.

ONNESHA. Y'all really talking about marriage?

SMITHY. Yo let the man be on his committed shit yo.

ONNESHA. I'm just sayin.

SMITHY. That's mad honorable.

ONNESHA. I'm just saying, that's pretty intense.

DWAYNE. She's worth it.

    She's like…the other half of my soul.

    I can feel it.

SEJAL. You must be really sad, too. About Gemma.

DWAYNE. Yeah.

       (**DWAYNE** *is struggling a little with the tie.* **SMITHY** *has ceremoniously placed a bottle in a brown paper bag amid the red cups, then goes to help* **DWAYNE** *with his tie.*)

SEJAL. (*Chewing it over.*) "Softens your grief…"

    Is she…gonna be in there? Is Gemma gonna be in there?

ONNESHA. Yeah, dumbass, that's what happens at a wake.

SEJAL. I dunno, yo, I never knew anybody who died!

ONNESHA. You never seen a movie, you never seen a movie where they got the casket and everything?

SEJAL. Not everything happens in life like happens in the movies, like you ever seen *Finding Nemo* yo? Fish don't talk / aight fish don't talk do they?

ONNESHA. Aight aight aight fish don't talk but yeah they gonna have her in there.

> *(A breath as they all really understand that, maybe for the first time.* **SMITHY** *finishes* **DWAYNE***'s tie.)*

I dunno if they're gonna, like, show her, though. Like if we'll see her.

DWAYNE. She didn't look good toward the end. Or, not not good, that doesn't matter. She didn't look like herself. So, nah, they're not gonna show her.

SEJAL. Good. Or, no, I don't mean good. I dunno what I mean.

DWAYNE. Ally's parents have been really – They're really like –

Graceful

Wow I sound mad weird yo…

SMITHY. You don't.

DWAYNE. Yeah, nah, yeah they been mad graceful.

I wanna be like them when I'm a parent.

> *(They all stand there for a breath.)*

SMITHY. Yo let's make this toast.

> *(***SMITHY*** *begins pouring a shot's worth into each red cup.)*

SEJAL. Yo Smithy, you just look old enough that they let you buy that? Or your older cousin get it for you, Smithy? Yo Smithy you got a fake? Yo if you got a fake, / could I get a fake?

ONNESHA. Oh my god, be quiet, Sejal! We tryna have a moment, yo!

> *(***SMITHY*** *distributes the cups. They all look around cautiously, making sure they're alone.)*

SMITHY. You wanna say something? Like a little speech?

DWAYNE. That's funny. Cuz Ally's saying something tonight. She asked me what she should say about Gemma.

SMITHY. And what you tell her?

DWAYNE. You know…just to be honest, and speak from her heart, and like capture a memory.

SMITHY. Aight so you wanna do that now?

(**DWAYNE** *thinks for a moment.*)

DWAYNE. Nah I don't wanna get all emotional. To Gemma.

(*They all echo this, then toast.* **SMITHY** *shoots the drink straight back — winces, but has done this before.* **ONNESHA** *has a pretty rough time with it, and* **SEJAL** *seems as if he has been poisoned.*)

SEJAL. Oh my god, oh my god, is this supposed to happen?

(*The others laugh at* **SEJAL** *through their wincing and coughing.*)

Nah yo for real I don't think this is supposed to happen!

(**SMITHY** *pats* **SEJAL**'*s back, then starts cleaning up.* **DWAYNE** *is looking up at the sky. He takes a picture of it with his phone.*)

ONNESHA. Oh, damn the moon.

SEJAL. That's ill when you can see it during the day.

(**DWAYNE** *observes the moon for another breath, then starts heading out.*)

DWAYNE. Aight yo let's do this.

(**SMITHY** *follows immediately, resolutely.*)

SEJAL. Damn he said aight let's do this and he was off like on a mission.

(**ONNESHA** *is smirking at* **SEJAL**.)

What, yo?

ONNESHA. Miracle of Life.

(**SEJAL** *groans in embarrassed frustration, and the two go off after the others.*)

3.

(Sun sets. Night, after the wake. **JENNY** *and* **TAMMY** *are on the roof, divvying out candy and snacks and sodas from plastic bags — an elaborate routine of portions and shares.)*

JENNY. I feel like such an idiot.

TAMMY. Well, don't.

JENNY. I wish it was that easy, like, "Yes I will feel this now, and no I will not feel that now."
But I feel what I feel,

TAMMY. Don't take all the Skittles.

JENNY. and I feel like an idiot.

TAMMY. I want the green ones.

JENNY. I thought Ally would wanna laugh, ya know? It was like we were trapped in this box of sadness.

TAMMY. That's a good description of a wake, yeah.

JENNY. Yeah! And I thought Ally is so funny, and fun, and Gemma wouldn't want her to be so sad.

TAMMY. Dead people don't want things.

JENNY. Oh my God, Tammy.

TAMMY. Wanting things is something you stop doing when you're dead.

JENNY. I said she wouldn't want her to be so sad, like, as a conjecture.
And I know Ally loves watching Vines, and she loves that goofy blonde guy who does the Vines, and we watched that one at lunch, so I pulled out my phone so she could watch it.

TAMMY. And she laughed, she did laugh.

JENNY. Yeah, then her Mom and Dad like scowled at us.

TAMMY. They didn't scowl, no one scowled.

JENNY. Yeah, and her aunts and uncles and grandparents and everyone scowled at us.
And I embarrassed her at her sister's wake. Which is like, which is like unthinkably stupid.

(*They take a couple breaths, sip sodas, watch the skyline.*)

TAMMY. Look, Jenny, not all families handle death like our family.

JENNY. I know.

TAMMY. Like when someone dies in our family, people grab guitars and sing songs and shit.

JENNY. Seriously.

TAMMY. We're weird, ya know? Like Uncle Jimmy's memorial was like one of the funnest / days –

JENNY. Funnest days we've ever had with the family, I was just thinking that!

TAMMY. Uh-huh, we're a weird hippy family who doesn't know how to deal with death / so we

JENNY. What?

TAMMY. pretend to worship life and love and the sun or whatever,

JENNY. I don't think that's true.

TAMMY. and that's not how all families do it. Ally's family needs to be sad and serious, that's how they're doing it.

JENNY. I don't think we don't know how to deal with death.

TAMMY. No one does. That's why humans came up with a billion different ways to do it, because no one's figured it out yet. And you're not an idiot because of that. You're a good friend. Ally knows that.

(**JENNY** *nods, gratefully.*)

JENNY. Little kids shouldn't get cancer.

TAMMY. Nope. If you got cancer –

JENNY. Oh my god, seriously?

TAMMY. I'm just saying if you got cancer, I hope I'd be as good of a sister for you as Ally was for Gemma.

JENNY. I think you would be.

TAMMY. I hope I die before you.

JENNY. No it has to be me, it definitely has to be me, I can't do this life thing without you.

I really can't. You can't have all the gummy bears!

TAMMY. I'm only taking the green ones!

JENNY. You say you're taking the green ones then you take all of them!

> (ALLY *enters with* KATHERINE, *mid-conversation, and their friend* SAM *follows them, carrying a portable speaker.*)

ALLY. But like, that's what I don't get about the soulmate thing.

KATHERINE. I think people define it differently.

ALLY. Yeah that's what I don't get. Like if there can be different definitions, then it's a perspective thing, it's not a soul thing. *(To* JENNY *and* TAMMY.*)* Hey, you got up here okay?

TAMMY. Yeah the doorman loves us.

JENNY. We're always over here copying Dwayne's Earth Science reports so he knows us.

Your speech was beautiful.

ALLY. No, it really wasn't.

KATHERINE. She can't take a compliment.

ALLY. I'll take a compliment when I deserve it, I don't deserve this one. *(Of the bags of snacks.)* You got the spicy chips?

> (TAMMY *digs them out and gives them to her.*)

SAM. You think he'll mind if we play music up here?

ALLY. Who?

SAM. Dwayne. He's gonna be up here in like two minutes.

ALLY. Don't worry about Dwayne.

SAM. Okay…but we're on his roof, so…

ALLY. Play the music if you want yo.

> (SAM *shrugs and puts on some music.*)

TAMMY. Are you and Dwayne doing okay?

KATHERINE. She's worried they don't talk about things the same way.

ALLY. Like if someone is the mate to your soul, then you should be able to talk to them about anything.

SAM. Maybe you could learn to talk.

KATHERINE. Yeah, maybe your souls have to grow together.

ALLY. Do souls grow? Is that something a soul can do?

SAM. I hope so! I mean I want my soul to grow. Is the music too loud?

ALLY. Stop worrying and just play the music.

KATHERINE. I don't think you guys need to know how to talk about everything all at once. You can teach him how you need him to listen.

ALLY. I don't wanna have to teach someone that.

> *(Abruptly,* **DWAYNE** *enters the roof, followed by* **ONNESHA, SEJAL,** *and* **SMITHY.** **ONNESHA** *and* **SEJAL** *will break off to the side under the following to get a round of selfie Snapchats going.)*

DWAYNE. Yo keep the music down!

SAM. See, I told you!

DWAYNE. Nah, it's just we're only six floors up, so the cops can hear from the street.

SMITHY. Hey I loved your speech. It was really brave.

ALLY. Can we not talk about that?

SMITHY. Oh, my bad.

ALLY. No, it's fine. I just came here to…not talk about that.

SMITHY. True, true, that's cool.

> *(An awkward breath all around.* **KATHERINE** *stays close to* **ALLY** *and forges ahead:)*

KATHERINE. Hey who's actually going to that assembly tomorrow?

SMITHY. Yo that assembly's stupid.

DWAYNE. Whoa, whoa, harsh words.

SAM. But we have to go to the assembly!

SEJAL. Yeah isn't it mandatory?

SAM. Yeah they're gonna take attendance, Smithy.

SMITHY. Nah, I don't need nobody telling me what books I can and can't read.

TAMMY. That's not what it's about!

KATHERINE. Yeah it's more about like – sensitivity, and appreciation –

SMITHY. I'mma read what I wanna read.

TAMMY. It's not like a censorship assembly, it's about trigger warnings.

DWAYNE. Oh word, Ally and I were reading about that the other day, how colleges are all bugging about trigger warnings now. *(To ALLY.)* Right?

SAM. But really Smithy, you're already in trouble with Mr. McGuire and this is like his thing, the trigger warning thing, so you have to go,

ALLY. Sam.

SAM. you have to go because he'll like call your parents and stuff!

ALLY. Yo Sam why don't you just worry about you and let other people worry about them.

(Another tense breath.)

JENNY. You okay?

(ALLY nods.)

SAM. I know I wasn't really invited…

ALLY. It's not you. It's all good. Keep talking. I said it's all good, / keep talking!

KATHERINE. Yeah so I wanna hear what they're gonna say at the assembly.

Because some books do upset me but sometimes I wanna be upset, ya know?

TAMMY. Catharsis. I want catharsis.

DWAYNE. Nah but sometimes the people teaching the stuff ain't all that sensitive.

I understand the kids at those colleges wanting to protest.

SEJAL. I don't wanna go to a school where everyone's protesting all the time.

KATHERINE. It's not all the time.

ONNESHA. You don't wanna go to school at all!

SEJAL. Yes I do!

ONNESHA. You just wanna like stuff on Instagram all day.

SEJAL. You're the one who started Snapchatting! And I wanna go to University of Miami. They got Marine Biology.

ONNESHA. What, like, studying whales?

SAM. How you gonna study whales, Sejal? Whales got the Miracle of Life too!

SEJAL. I left the class because I knew that stuff already! Oh my God!

(Everyone laughs.)

DWAYNE. *(To* **JENNY** *and* **TAMMY***.)* Yo are you two gonna go to the same school?

(The sisters glance at each other nervously.)

Oh my bad, is that like…?

TAMMY. No, it's cool, it's just people ask us that a lot.

JENNY. And we don't really know what we wanna do.

DWAYNE. You both wanna do music, right?

JENNY. Yeah so if we were both in the same department, it might get a little…

TAMMY. Claustrophobic. But she's looking at Ithaca for Music Education.

JENNY. And she's looking more at Cornell for performance – she has the grades for Cornell.

TAMMY. So I'd be just down the hill.

DWAYNE. That's a good solution! Me and Ally are thinking of something similar, like if we go to schools in cities near each other. Then we can drive to visit each other and everything.

> (**ALLY** *just sits off to the side with* **KATHERINE**, *not responding.*)

SMITHY. I wonder where my Basic Training's gonna be.

ONNESHA. Basic Training?

SMITHY. My family's all military yo, like three generations back yo, we all soldiers.
So, I gotta take a test called an ASVAB, and that'll tell me what I'm good at.
Then that'll tell them what base to put me at.

ONNESHA. That's crazy. I'm jealous of you.

SAM. You jealous of him going off to the army?

ONNESHA. I'm jealous of anyone who has an option, yo. My Dad owns a restaurant. Day after graduation he's dropping me off to shadow the maître d'!

DWAYNE. He ain't even gonna wait that long!

SEJAL. Yeah, like right after graduation, you're still gonna be in your cap and gown –

ONNESHA. Shut up.

SAM. Yeah and he's gonna drop you off right in the kitchen like that.

DWAYNE. Diploma in ya hand and everything.

ONNESHA. Shut up, yo!

> (**ONNESHA** *goes to the stash of snacks and grabs some popcorn.* **SEJAL** *joins her.*)

DWAYNE. You gonna have to come visit at school though.

ONNESHA. Whatever.

SAM. Nah for real. I'm probably going to Rutgers, 'cause everyone in my family goes there.
We'll get you on a train and you'll come visit.

DWAYNE. Yeah yo. I'll come with you, we'll make it like a little ritual with everybody.

ONNESHA. Nope, I don't need to visit any students, I'm gonna be working, thank you very much!

*(They all chuckle – **SEJAL** and **ONNESHA** are taking turns throwing popcorn kernels and catching them with their mouths.)*

*(**SMITHY** and has moved over to the portable speaker and is bobbing his head to the music.)*

*(**ALLY** has been observing them all having fun.)*

(She is crying quietly.)

*(**KATHERINE** has noticed, and is discreetly keeping a steady hand on her shoulder.)*

*(**JENNY** and **TAMMY** join them.)*

(The others begin to notice.)

(Their laughter quiets down.)

(They all stand there, the music playing softly.)

*(**DWAYNE** is like a deer in headlights. **SMITHY** gently pushes at his back to urge him to go comfort **ALLY**.)*

*(**DWAYNE** sits with her. He holds her hand. She lets him. She buries her face into **KATHERINE**'s shoulder.)*

*(Just the sounds of the city, and the light of the passing moon, as the friends stay with **ALLY**.)*

4.

(The night of the blood moon.)

*(***ALLY***'s here, watching the eclipse begin.)*

*(***DWAYNE*** rushes out onto the roof, fumbling with a camera. He stops short, seeing ***ALLY***.)*

ALLY. It's a reflection.

DWAYNE. What's a reflection?

ALLY. I looked it up. It looks red because it's reflecting the red from our atmosphere back to us. Like how it reflects the sun usually, but tonight it's gonna reflect, like, us, back to us.

DWAYNE. That's so cool.

ALLY. It still doesn't look red though.

DWAYNE. Nah, because, yeah, it's the eclipse first, then it'll turn red.
Like that's our shadow. Like us and everybody and everything, that's our shadow.

(They observe for a moment.)

ALLY. *(Of the camera.)* You upgraded, huh?

DWAYNE. My uncle let me borrow it.

(They watch the eclipse for some breaths.)

ALLY. It was unfair of me. To ask you what to say at the wake.

DWAYNE. Not unfair.

ALLY. Sort of like an impossible thing to ask of someone, yeah.

DWAYNE. I got angry cuz I couldn't help.

ALLY. I know.

DWAYNE. The thing I said about people getting old.

ALLY. No, it's

DWAYNE. I shoulda thought before I said it.

ALLY. No, it's fine. You're allowed to say what you're thinking. A lotta things are gonna make me sad about Gemma, like forever, so I can't get mad every time someone says something that makes me think of her.

DWAYNE. But I was thinking. Gemma will grow old, kinda.

ALLY. How?

DWAYNE. You gonna take her with you. I'mma – I'mma take her with me. So, like, with us. She'll get old.

ALLY. No. She won't.

> (**DWAYNE** *is frustrated, but works through it and diverts it into:*)

DWAYNE. If we have a daughter, we could like
We could name her, like
I mean only if you want to, only if that would make you feel like
It'll be important that our kids know they have an aunt, or had an aunt, or have had an aunt, and who she was. That's important.

> (**DWAYNE** *focuses his camera, and snaps some shots of the moon.* **ALLY** *observes him for some breaths, then:*)

ALLY. Promise me something, okay?

DWAYNE. Promise you what.

ALLY. That you won't like, associate this with Gemma.

DWAYNE. Associate what?

ALLY. Because like Gemma is like – unchanging now?
She is...completed...or –
I dunno but like anything that we feel right now, we're gonna look back and like, and like
Gah, I fucking hate –

DWAYNE. Um, I don't know what you...

ALLY. I fucking hate how no one has made the words for this yet, no one has – defined, like –
Everything we feel in these moments, when we're older, we're gonna look back and Gemma will look like those

feelings. So when you're like fifty-four or whatever, don't think about this and remember Gemma differently because you see her in this. Promise.

DWAYNE. Promise.

> *(A breath or two. They both know their lives about to change, but not how.)*

ALLY. I feel like – I feel like I don't know what my life is gonna be, like
You know how the people who don't know if there's a God or not, like

DWAYNE. Agnostics.

ALLY. Agnostics, they can't say one way or the other if there's a God or what God is.
I'm like agnostic about my life yo.

DWAYNE. Ally.

ALLY. Like I don't know if my life is gonna be one thing or another,

DWAYNE. Ally, yo.

ALLY. or what my life is even, and, and

DWAYNE. You're worrying me.

ALLY. and I feel like I owe it to Gemma, I owe it to Gemma to not, like,

DWAYNE. Ally, wait.

ALLY. to not like box my life into some pre-determined model, to not like predict my own life then try to live inside the prediction.

> *(She is breaking up with him:)*

I feel like I need some time to figure things out on my own.

> *(He is trying not to cry.)*

DWAYNE. Can I ask something?

ALLY. No.

DWAYNE. You don't know what I'm gonna ask.

ALLY. Yeah, I do.

DWAYNE. Try not to predict ya life then live inside the /
  prediction, Ally.

ALLY. Shut up yo.

DWAYNE. Is there anything I can / do differently?

ALLY. No.

DWAYNE. But if I just – if I was different a little, then

ALLY. No.

> (DWAYNE *nods, going somewhere deep inside his*
> *head. He pops out of it:*)

DWAYNE. Fuck, you just broke up with me on our /
  anniversary yo.

ALLY. I know.

DWAYNE. Like this day is always gonna have some resonance
  on the calendar / for me yo.

ALLY. I know, oh my god, I'm sorry.

> (*A couple breaths.*)

DWAYNE. This is the worst feeling I've ever felt.

> (ALLY *nods, appreciating that. They sit together for*
> *a few long breaths.*)

ALLY. How far the ocean goes down.

DWAYNE. Ocean what?

ALLY. Where the bottom of the ocean is. What kinda life
  can live at the bottom.

DWAYNE. Ally, what?

ALLY. Things you can still find out about the world. You
  said there's nothing left to find out.
  If atoms can really be two places at once.

DWAYNE. Why whale calls are getting lower and lower each
  year.

ALLY. Where the whales go for most of their lives.

DWAYNE. Why we sleep.

ALLY. What parts of our brain make us ourselves.

DWAYNE. How to stop cancer.

(**ALLY** *pauses for a moment, touched.*)

ALLY. I hope you find that out. Find that out, okay?

DWAYNE. Okay.

(*They smile sadly at each other.* **ALLY** *glances upward.*)

ALLY. Oh wow.

DWAYNE. Oh shit.

ALLY. Oh wow. It's so…

DWAYNE. I know.

ALLY. It's so…

(*She doesn't have the words. They breathe in and out for several moments, awestruck.*)

End of Play

LANDLINES

Hannah Bos & Paul Thureen

LANDLINES was first presented by Keen Company (Jonathan Silverstein, Artistic Director; Mark Armstrong, Director of New Work) and Samuel French, Inc. as part of the 2016 Keen Teens Festival of New Work from May 13-15. The performance was directed by Liz Carlson. The cast was as follows:

ANNOUNCER 1	Marcel Isaiah Martinez
ANNOUNCER 2	Marissa Harris
DIRECTOR	Victor Vegas
VOLUNTEER A	Victor Vegas
VOLUNTEER B	Brooke Hamke
VOLUNTEER C	Kate Semmens
VOLUNTEER D	Maya Pagan
BEEP	Darren Valdera
BOP	Jennifer Perskin
POLICEWOMAN	Kate Semmens
MAKE-UP PERSON	Brooke Hamke
IRISH PERSON	Kate Semmens
OLD WOMAN	Maya Pagan
OLD MAN	Victor Vegas
CHILD	Brooke Hamke
TEENAGE BOY	Roza Chervinsky
TEENAGE GIRL	Maya Pagan
CAT	Roza Chervinsky

CHARACTERS

ANNOUNCER 1 – Co-host of a TV telethon

ANNOUNCER 2 – Co-host of a TV telethon

DIRECTOR – Director of the TV telethon

VOLUNTEER A – Telethon Volunteer

VOLUNTEER B – Telethon Volunteer

VOLUNTEER C – Telethon Volunteer

VOLUNTEER D – Telethon Volunteer

BEEP – You remember Beep! The furry creature
from that famous kids show!

BOP – You remember Bop! The other furry creature
from that famous kids show!

Characters below can be double, triple, or even quadruple cast or played by individual actors. Basically everyone other than the Announcers and Beep and Bop can play multiple characters. We think it would be cool if Teenage Girl and Old Woman were played by the same person doing different voices. Any gender can play any character! Don't worry about stage directions specifying "him" and "her."

POLICEWOMAN

MAKE-UP PERSON

IRISH PERSON

OLD WOMAN

OLD MAN

CHILD – 6-ish years old

TEENAGE BOY

TEENAGE GIRL

CAT

AUTHOR'S NOTES

The scenes in the dark should be done in as close to total darkness as possible. Though…it might be fun if you can just barely see a glimpse of the end of the Teenage Girl and Old Woman conversation if it is indeed played by the same person. Your call!

Don't play things with a "wink." When in doubt, err on the side of dryness (especially the cat…make that guy super dry). Announcers should be bright and exuberant. Don't rush the lines too much, but for the most part cues should be picked up very quickly for a fun, seamless banter.

Dedicated to Telephones.

*(A TV studio during a fundraising telethon for a public television style TV network. **TWO ANNOUNCERS** with microphones. A director watching from the wings. A table in the background with four volunteers quietly taking phone calls from people pledging money.)*

ANNOUNCER 1. That's right Ron, it *is* certainly "a day to walk in the park" as they say on that show on the TV in your home or the electronics store where you are killing time in the rain…that we are interrupting right now. Today we have an incredible offer for those of you making pledges. We are giving away –

ANNOUNCER 2: Speaking of this award winning show and interrupting…

ANNOUNCER 1. We couldn't have programs like this –

ANNOUNCER 2. With people with accents from other countries –

ANNOUNCER 1. Without viewers like you listening with your normal accent at home.

ANNOUNCER 2. Noticing how funny they sound.

ANNOUNCER 1. Maybe they eat different food than you do.

ANNOUNCER 2. Maybe they are getting up when you are going to sleep at night.

ANNOUNCER 1. Maybe they are having a bad day.

ANNOUNCER 2. Or a bad year.

ANNOUNCER 1. Things just aren't going their way.

ANNOUNCER 2. So pick up the phone.

ANNOUNCER 1. Give us a call.

ANNOUNCER 2. Take a minute and pick up the phone or hammer and –

ANNOUNCER 1. Dial the number you see on the bottom of your screen right there.

ANNOUNCER 2. Between the top edge of your television and your floor.

ANNOUNCER 1. Our Volunteers are gonna be here all night.

ANNOUNCER 2. Waiting for your call.

ANNOUNCER 1. Or at least for the next twenty minutes.

ANNOUNCER 2. So make a pledge today and give us a hello.

ANNOUNCER 1. Hello.

ANNOUNCER 2. Hi.

ANNOUNCER 1. Hi.

ANNOUNCER 2. Hi! Who is this on the line?

> *(Somewhere to the side we see a* **POLICEWOMAN** *on a phone.)*

POLICEWOMAN. 911 can I help you?

ANNOUNCER 2. Is this an emergency?

POLICEWOMAN. I'm asking you.

ANNOUNCER 2. Are you ok?

POLICEWOMAN. Are you?

ANNOUNCER 2. I think so.

POLICEWOMAN. Good.

> *(The* **POLICEWOMAN** *hangs up. Dial tone.)*

ANNOUNCER 2. That was nice.

ANNOUNCER 1. *(Finger to ear.)* I'm getting a nudge from Carol that we are running low on time.

ANNOUNCER 2. We're just asking for money.

ANNOUNCER 1. And for you to dial the phone.

DIRECTOR. AND BREAK!

> *(The* **ANNOUNCERS** *relax as a* **MAKE-UP PERSON** *comes onto the stage.)*

MAKE-UP PERSON. I'm just going to put on a little powder and cream so you don't look like you. Don't worry you won't recognize yourself.

DIRECTOR. Give him a little something to make his face pop.

MAKE-UP PERSON. You got it!

>   (**MAKE-UP PERSON** *puts a lot of blush on both*
>   **ANNOUNCERS**' *cheeks.*)

ANNOUNCER 1. Did you find your cat ever?

ANNOUNCER 2. Yeah, she came back but then she left again.

ANNOUNCER 1. I don't get it.

ANNOUNCER 2. She forgot some of her things.

MAKE-UP PERSON. Oh yeah. That's looking good.

ANNOUNCER 1. You don't think it's too much?

MAKE-UP PERSON. You should see the other guy!

ANNOUNCER 2. I'm right here.

MAKE-UP PERSON. Can you go like this *(Makes a weird face.)*
and close your eyes for me honey?

>   (**ANNOUNCER 2** *copies the weird face and*
>   *closes his eyes.* **MAKE-UP PERSON** *walks away.*
>   **ANNOUNCER 2** *is still making a weird face.*)

DIRECTOR. And we are back in five ... four ... three ...
two ...

ANNOUNCER 1. One thing we like to do is hear from people
like you.

ANNOUNCER 2. Let's take a listen to some more calls!

>   (**ANNOUNCER 2** *opens eyes and drops weird face.*
>   *The* **ANNOUNCERS** *walk behind the long table of*
>   *volunteers and stand listening to their phone calls.*
>   *They bend over and get a little too close.*)

VOLUNTEER A. I'm so glad you are a fan.

>   *(Somewhere to the side we see an* **OLD WOMAN** *on*
>   *a phone.)*

OLD WOMAN. I don't want a fan. I want –

VOLUNTEER A. So happy that you are calling in today. How
much would you like to pledge this evening?

OLD WOMAN. I want the mug.

VOLUNTEER A. Just a sec! *(Covering phone, whispering.)* Do
we have mugs?

VOLUNTEER B. Nope, not tonight.

VOLUNTEER C. Offer her a calendar or a mouse.

VOLUNTEER A. We have a colander and mice.

OLD WOMAN. Nah, I want a mug. I've been drinking out of bowls.

>   *(She hangs up. Dial tone.)*

VOLUNTEER D. Hello! So happy to have you on the line.

>   *(To the side: a child on a rug talking on a phone.)*

CHILD. I would like to speak to Beep or Bop.

VOLUNTEER D. Who?

CHILD. Beep or Bop. The red guy and the blue one.

VOLUNTEER D. Their show's not on right now.

CHILD. But –

VOLUNTEER D. That's a morning show.

CHILD. Can you give them a message?

VOLUNTEER D. No. They're not real.

>   *(Gasps!)*

VOLUNTEER A. Oh no!

VOLUNTEER B. Shh!

CHILD. They're not?

>   *(**BEEP** and **BOP** – two strange, large furry creatures [characters from a kids show], one red and one blue, large eyeballs – enter from out of nowhere.)*

BEEP AND BOP. WE'RE NOT?

>   *(They look at the **ANNOUNCERS**, who shake their heads. They look at each other.)*

BEEP. Did you know?

>   *(**BOP** looks down sheepishly.)*

Look at me, Bop.

>   *(He can't.)*

BOP. No.

BEEP. Did you know, Bop?

BOP. Maybe.

BEEP. You knew we weren't real?

> (**BOP** *looks at* **BEEP**. *Beat.*)

BOP. …Yes.

BEEP. How come you never told me all these years. All that we have been through. All the numbers and colors we learned. All the songs about sharing. And rhymes.

BOP. I just didn't have it in me. You were so happy, Beep.

> (**BEEP** *is devastated.*)

BEEP. Is it true?

BOP. Knock Knock?

BEEP. Who's there?

ANNOUNCER 1. And there goes your childhood!

> (**BEEP** *and* **BOP** *sadly retreat off stage.*)

What is so great about today is that with every pledge you will get this *Celtic Sounds of Ireland* CD set with a retail value of over one hundred and fifty dollars.

ANNOUNCER 2. Tell us about the Sounds of Ireland CD.

> (*An* **IRISH PERSON** *walks onto the stage and stands by the* **ANNOUNCERS**.)

IRISH PERSON. (*Irish accent.*) We have some of the same sounds you guys have here. Train sounds, bird sounds, car horns and the occasional bark from a neighbor's dog. We have foghorns and mopeds. I guess you all call them scooters and such. Our babies sound the same as yours, until eventually they don't. They grow up and they sound Irish. Yeah.

ANNOUNCERS 1 AND 2. Looking forward to giving that a listen! …Jinx!

DIRECTOR. AND BREAK!

> (**BEEP** *and* **BOP** *are back.* **BEEP** *is having a panic attack and breathing into a small paper bag.*)

BEEP. We used to do Jinx.

BOP. No. We called the game "Ditto"?

BEEP. Ditto?

BOP. Yeah.

BEEP. I thought it was –

BOP AND BEEP. Jinx… Jinx!

BEEP. *(Sadly.)* You owe me Coke.

BOP. Ok. I will get you that Coke. You won fair and square.

(**BEEP** *and* **BOP** *walk off stage.*)

DIRECTOR. And we are back in five, four, three, two…

(*Lights fade to black. The* **DIRECTOR***'s voice is now amplified and somehow different. It gets slower and slower.*)

(*Voiceover.*) One, zero, negative one, negative two, negative three, negative four, negative five, negative six.

(*Complete darkness and silence. Then we hear:*)

TEENAGE BOY. Um… Where am I?

TEENAGE GIRL. I don't know.

TEENAGE BOY. Ahhh! Sorry. I didn't know there was someone else here.

TEENAGE GIRL. I didn't either.

TEENAGE BOY. How long have you been here?

TEENAGE GIRL. Great question. It's hard to tell in here… Maybe since I was thirteen?

TEENAGE BOY. How old are you now?

TEENAGE GIRL. Great question. I think still something that ends with a "teen" maybe. But it's hard to tell. It felt like my birthday about what feels like four months ago. I wonder what I look like now.

TEENAGE BOY. What did you look like *then*?

TEENAGE GIRL. Great question. My grandma said I looked like one of her sisters. She thought that was funny, because I was actually named after her *other* sister.

TEENAGE BOY. What's your name?

TEENAGE GIRL. Teenage Girl. Weird right? Oh…and *GREAT* question. Hey, here's a story for you. I called my grandparents' place on the telephone one time. Well, I mean I used to call their place all the time. I would call my grandmother twice a week just to chat with her. Tell her about my life. Tell her about my friends or boys. I would change a few things in case. I didn't want to freak her out. Not that I did anything bad but I tried a cigarette once and I didn't tell her. She would tell me about her day and her friends and their grandchildren. She would ask me if I needed money and I would say no and then she would send me a check a few days later for five dollars. I would make her laugh and she would tell me how proud she was of me. I loved hearing her stories about the past and how different it was growing up in her home country. But anyway… I was going to tell you about this ONE time I called my grandparents place. This is when I was twelve. My grandparents died when I was eleven. But I called them anyway and just let it ring and ring and ring. They didn't have an answering machine, they were too old for such new things. So I knew that it would just ring and ring and ring forever. And it rang and rang and rang forever. *(Beat.)* They didn't die at the same time by the way. Just the same year.

TEENAGE BOY. Hey Teenage Girl?

TEENAGE GIRL. Yeah?

TEENAGE BOY. My name is Teenage Boy. I wonder if we're related or something. Like brother and sister maybe.

TEENAGE GIRL. Wow. I wonder if you look like me and our Great Aunt?

TEENAGE BOY. What was her name?

TEENAGE GIRL. Old Woman. There were three sisters. Old Woman (who looks like me and you), Teenage Girl (who I was named after) and then Myrtle (our grandma).

VOICE OF THE IRISH PERSON. My name's Brandon by the way.

TEENAGE BOY AND TEENAGE GIRL. Ahhhh!

IRISH PERSON. I'm from Ireland.

TEENAGE GIRL. Are we in *Ireland?*

IRISH PERSON. It's really hard to tell from the sounds.

> *(Faint but kinda scary low, ethereal groaning sound.)*

…I'd guess… No? Maybe… Belize?

ANNOUNCER 1. Belize is sunny though.

TEENAGE BOY, TEENAGE GIRL, IRISH PERSON. Ahhhhhh!

ANNOUNCER 1. Sorry.

TEENAGE BOY. Who are you?

ANNOUNCER 1. I'm Announcer 1.

IRISH PERSON. Where are we?

ANNOUNCER 1. *(Mysteriously.)* In the bowels.

TEENAGE GIRL. Of…?

ANNOUNCER 1. *(Mysteriously.)* A whale. *(Beat.)* Kidding. The TV studio. You know, this studio used to have live audiences back in the day. They'd film a lot of the TV programs here. People would send letters requesting tickets to an address on the bottom of the screen. This was even before Internet. Sometimes they would call a number too. And leave their name on a phone machine. Someone at the TV studio would play back the tape on that phone machine and listen to all the names of families with kids that would be trying to get in to see a live taping. The clown show in particular got to be so popular that there was a waitlist of five years. Kids would watch at home and see the clown's magic tricks and perfect puns and all the whipped cream eating. And it culminated with the Grand Prize of a red wagon if a kid was lucky enough to throw the ball into the fishbowl. And those kids watching at home would run and tell their Moms and Dads to get them on the waitlist for tickets. By the time the Moms and Dads got the call years later, a lot of kids had grown out of wanting to see the clown show. Isn't that sad?

(Lights up and **OLD WOMAN** *is sitting at a table with her husband,* **OLD MAN**. *They drink coffee out of bowls.)*

OLD WOMAN. More coffee?

OLD MAN. Maybe just half a bowl.

(She uses her walker to [slooooowly] cross the stage to the coffee pot… Why is it so far away?! Who knows. She [sloooooowly] makes her way back to the table with the coffee pot. Begins to pour…and realizes there's no coffee left in the pot [best not to have a clear coffee pot for this to be a surprise].)

OLD WOMAN. I'll brew some more. I could use another bowl.

(She uses her walker to cross the stage. Even slower than before. She's exhausted. This time they talk during the long journey.)

OLD MAN. I heard you on the telephone earlier.

OLD WOMAN. I called in to that telethon.

OLD MAN. What did they say?

OLD WOMAN. I got on the air.

OLD MAN. What did they say?

OLD WOMAN. They don't have any more mugs but they have a *mouse* problem.

OLD MAN. Disgusting.

OLD WOMAN. Must have left food out.

OLD MAN. Do they live above a restaurant?

OLD WOMAN. No, it's a TV studio.

OLD MAN. Oh. I wish we lived above a restaurant. I'm hungry.

OLD WOMAN. There's a leftover sandwich.

(The **OLD MAN** *gets up with his walker and walks [slooooowly] to the sandwich, which we now see, and is somewhere far away from where* **OLD WOMAN** *is walking with the coffee pot. Why*

is everything so far away? They both walk so so slowly away from each other. As they walk:)

OLD MAN. What kind of sandwich is it?

OLD WOMAN. I know what you like.

OLD MAN. Roast beef?

OLD WOMAN. I know all the things you like and don't like and what is good for you and what will make you last.

OLD MAN. *(A little disappointed.)* Oh…then it's turkey.

OLD WOMAN. I put cheese on though.

OLD MAN. Good… Mayo?

OLD WOMAN. Not good for you.

OLD MAN. I liked when we didn't have to care about those things. I liked when I could have whatever I wanted between two slices.

OLD WOMAN. Those were the days.

OLD MAN. It's funny to think, that after all these years –

OLD WOMAN. We just got married last summer.

OLD MAN. I wasn't going to say something about us. But since you brought it up. This has been the best half-year of my long life.

OLD WOMAN. I feel the same way. Maybe that's why my mother named me Old Woman. She knew that that's when I'd really come into my own. When I became the age my name said I was.

> **(OLD MAN** *has reached the sandwich.* **OLD WOMAN** *has reached the coffee table.)*

OLD MAN. I like walking and talking to you. *(Beat.)* What did I walk over here for anyway?

OLD WOMAN. Regular or Decaf, sweetheart?

OLD MAN. What time is it?

OLD WOMAN. Six. *(Beat.)* Five … four … three … two …

> *(Transition back to the TV studio. The* **OLD PEOPLE** *walk off slowly and the* **ANNOUNCERS** *and* **VOLUNTEERS** *return.)*

ANNOUNCER 1. And we're BACK!

ANNOUNCER 2. I'm sure you viewers at home are thinking…

ANNOUNCER 1 & 2. WHAT THE HECK IS GOING ON!?

ANNOUNCER 1. What am I watching?

ANNOUNCER 2. Why am I feeling things?

ANNOUNCER 1. Who are those old guys?

ANNOUNCER 2. How many characters are there?

ANNOUNCER 1. What number am I thinking of?

ANNOUNCER 2. No…they weren't thinking that.

ANNOUNCER 1. Oh. Well…this is just the kind of thought provoking programing we find so important and why you should…

ANNOUNCER 2. Pick up the phone.

ANNOUNCER 1. Give us a call.

ANNOUNCER 2. Take a minute and pick up the phone or hammer and –

ANNOUNCER 1. Dial the number you see on the bottom of your screen right there.

ANNOUNCER 2. Between the top edge of your television and your floor.

ANNOUNCER 1. We're gonna be here all night.

ANNOUNCER 2. Before those calls start flooding in…let's get to know our Volunteers!

(The **ANNOUNCERS** *walk to the Volunteer table.)*

ANNOUNCER 1. Tell us about yourselves!

(The **ANNOUNCERS** *hold out their microphones.)*

VOLUNTEER A. My name is Ryan and I'm getting extra credit for volunteering today. I told off my teacher to impress a girl who is now dating my best friend Jim. It wasn't worth it. But what I said was really funny. Can't remember but I know I made a lot of people laugh. I also have a pet rat who is depressed.

VOLUNTEER D. Hi. Everyone calls me Tatiana. I'm not sure why. My name is Maya.

VOLUNTEER C. Hey big fan of this channel. I love all its shows and I love watching TV. It's all I do. That doesn't make me dumb just a lot less smarter than everyone else I know. I'm an only child and my older brother is on the football team. What was the question?

VOLUNTEER B. My name is K. I'm pretty uncomfortable sharing any details about my life on live TV, so…um…

> *(Very long pause. She looks at the **ANNOUNCERS**. They clearly aren't going to let her off the hook. The **ANNOUNCERS** push their microphones in real close.)*

…I… I'm a person… I have wants and needs and things I like to do. I…buy things at stores. I…have a body, I'm not sure what else –

ANNOUNCER 2. Fantastic! Thanks guys! Now how 'bout just something you've never told anyone. Ever. Deepest darkest secret. Would love to hear from all of you.

> *(The **VOLUNTEERS** all say their things at the exact same time. **VOLUNTEER B**'s line trails on just a bit longer than everyone elses:)*

VOLUNTEER A. I saw a ghost at my summer camp.

VOLUNTEER D. I can name all fifty-eight states.

VOLUNTEER C. I love burgers!

VOLUNTEER B. I'm just really really *really* uncomfortable with this.

> *(All the phones start ringing. The **VOLUNTEERS** pick them up. Maybe they sing their "hellos" one after another to make a musical chord.)*

VOLUNTEER A. Hello!

VOLUNTEER B. Hello!

VOLUNTEER C. Hello!

VOLUNTEER D. Hello!

ALL VOLUNTEERS. HELLO!!

> *(They then go into [unheard] conversations on the phone.)*

ANNOUNCER 1. Beautiful! Remember to keep those calls coming in and as soon as we hit our pledge goal… *(To **ANNOUNCER 2**.)* What's our pledge goal again?

ANNOUNCER 2. It's the amount of money we hope to raise.

ANNOUNCER 1. Right! And then we'll get you back to your regularly scheduled programming!

ANNOUNCER 2. And now, all you lovely viewers at home, we have an EXTRA special treat…your favorite not reals… Beep and Bop! Singing the song "It's Beep and Bop" from the show "It's Beep and Bop"!

> *(Bouncy music starts. A spotlight, the rest of the stage in darkness. **BEEP** and **BOP**, sipping sodas, dejectedly walk into the light. **BOP** sings*. **BEEP** kinda mumbles along:)*

WE ARE REAL
REAL GOOD FRIENDS
NOT RECOGNIZABLE ANIMALS
BUT STILL YOUR FRIENDS
I AM BLUE
HE IS RED
TOGETHER WE MAKE
ONE RED GUY
AND ONE BLUE GUY
YOU JUST LEARNED COLORS.
WELL TWO BUT STILL.

BEEP. I can't do this.

> *(The music keeps playing under the following conversation.)*

BOP. That's ok, Bop. What do you want to do?

BEEP. What are my options?

BOP. Well…we could just stand here and talk, we could –

BEEP. Stand here and talk.

BOP. OK. Tell me how you feel. I'll listen.

BEEP. I feel sad. And scared. And… I *feel* like I'm real even though I guess I'm not.

---

*Licensees should create an original composition.

BOP. But you've made so many people happy.

BEEP. Really?

BOP. Yes!

BEEP. *Real* people?

BOP. ...Sure.

BEEP. And I feel like I lost my best friend. Because you're not real either.

BOP. You've been not real to me for years. But I still love you.

BEEP. Really?

BOP. Sure! You never really lose good friends. Even when things ebb and flow. You might grow out of something or think you are a different person or think they are a traitor and killed your whole family...well not that example, but true friends play in your mind forever.

BEEP. I feel like just getting highlights...or shaving all this fake fur off and seeing what's underneath!

BOP: I think it's a different person inside you.

BEEP. That's what I'm saying.

BOP. No, I mean...really there is another person inside you.

BEEP. OH GOD. OH GOD! ...You mean?

BOP. Yeah.

> (**BEEP** *looks down at himself. Pokes his belly. Twice.*)

BEEP. *(Tentatively.)* Hello? ...Hello?

> (*The spotlight goes out. Darkness. We hear the echo of* **BEEP**'s *voice from beyond.*)

TEENAGE GIRL. Hello? ...Hello? Who is that? Teenage Boy? ...Announcer 1? Guess it's back to just me again.

> (*Long beat of silence.*)

IRISH PERSON. No, I'm still here too.

TEENAGE GIRL. Ahhhhh!

IRISH PERSON. Sorry.

TEENAGE GIRL. S'ok. Hi Brandon.

IRISH PERSON. Hi.

TEENAGE GIRL. How are things over there?

IRISH PERSON. Oh, it reminds me of the nighttime in Ireland. People sleep. People dream. Some people kiss and make babies in the dark. But you can't really see unless you are looking. Not that I look. I respect people's privacy. I'm just saying it's romantic at times. Until it's not. Also, the mice come out. Sometimes bugs. Moles. Generally quiet until it's not. But that will get me rambling about sounds again. In all your time here…you ever encounter bugs or mice?

TEENAGE GIRL. Yeah, I was just asking if you were ok.

OLD WOMAN. Funny you should mention mice.

TEENAGE GIRL & IRISH PERSON. Ahhhhhhh!

TEENAGE GIRL. Sorry, I didn't know someone else was here.

OLD WOMAN. I was just talking about mice earlier today. With a nice young person on the telephone. And a nice Old Man while walking. Mint?

TEENAGE GIRL. Sure.

IRISH PERSON. Thanks.

> *(The loud sounds of unwrapping mints. They all eat mints. Distant sound of another* **BEEP***'s "Hello?")*

IRISH PERSON Weird.

TEENAGE GIRL. Yeah.

OLD WOMAN. What a funny place to end up. I'm trying to think back to where I was before this and I only remember the thing about the mice. Maybe… *(Very creepy voice.)* I've been dead for years. *(Regular old woman voice.)* I'm just kidding. Let's see…before the mice was coffee. And before that was…calling the telethon. And before that I got married. And before that I was a little girl named Old Woman.

TEENAGE GIRL. Huh.

OLD WOMAN. Yes, quite a life.

TEENAGE GIRL. I think you're my Great Aunt. My name is Teenage Girl. I was named after your sister. Your other sister Myrtle was my grandma.

OLD WOMAN. Well then you must be the one who looks like me.

TEENAGE GIRL. So they say. I wish you could have met my brother. You would have liked him. He looked like us too. He's gone now.

OLD WOMAN. I'm sorry dear.

TEENAGE GIRL. …Old Woman?

OLD WOMAN. Yes?

TEENAGE GIRL. I miss my grandma. Can I talk to you about friends and boys and when I smoked a cigarette? And can you tell me about your home country where you grew up?

OLD WOMAN. Of course my sweet.

IRISH PERSON. Aye, that's beautiful isn't it?

TEENAGE GIRL. I forgot you were here.

IRISH PERSON. Oh, well… I'll be leaving soon. Most likely in, I don't know. Five seconds?

TEENAGE GIRL. Five … four … three … two …

(Lights up. We're back in the studio!)

ANNOUNCER 2. Welcome back, folks!

ANNOUNCER 1. Our phones are still open.

ANNOUNCER 2. We really need people like you to pick up the phone.

ANNOUNCER 1. Give us a call!

ANNOUNCER 2. Give us your money!

ANNOUNCER 1. Give us your heart!

ANNOUNCER 2. Fight for what you believe in!

ANNOUNCER 1. This is what makes our country strong.

ANNOUNCER 2. Board up your windows and –

VOLUNTEER A. Hey Gary?

ANNOUNCER 2. …Yeah?

VOLUNTEER A. There is someone asking for you…and they found your cat?

ANNOUNCER 2. *(Stunned.)* …Really?

VOLUNTEER A. Yeah…they have her on the phone.

> *(**ANNOUNCER 2** apprehensively walks over to the phone and begins to speak into it.)*

ANNOUNCER 2. Hey.

> *(Somewhere to the side we see a cat on a phone. All Black costume. Face painted. Cat ears. Not sexy. Very dry delivery.)*

CAT. Hey.

ANNOUNCER 2. Hey.

> *(Silence. Everyone in the studio looks at them and then looks away not to be nosey.)*

You don't even call. I have to hear about you leaving from Phil.

CAT. I'm calling now.

ANNOUNCER 2. I miss us.

CAT. I do too Gary. I do too.

ANNOUNCER 2. I'm at work. Can you call me Announcer 2?

CAT. No one's listening are they?

> *(**ANNOUNCER 2** looks out at the audience.)*

ANNOUNCER 2. Everyone's listening. We're on a live telethon.

CAT. Ok. Announcer 2. I just… I needed to hear your voice.

ANNOUNCER 2. This is my voice.

CAT. Yup. That's your voice.

ANNOUNCER 2. Can I ask you something?

CAT. Sure… Just don't ask me where the body is.

ANNOUNCER 2. Would… *(Looks at everyone looking at him. Decides to ask something else.)* …You like to make a pledge?

CAT. I'm short on cash right now.

ANNOUNCER 1. Wow. Things just got *real* weird. Well, while they sort that out –

ANNOUNCER 2. Speaking of sorting out, I just hung up on my cat!

> (**CAT** *mopes away.*)

ANNOUNCER 1. *(Finger to ear.)* I'm getting word from Carol that we've just met our pledge goal!

ANNOUNCER 2. Really?!

ANNOUNCER 1. Yes, I have a thingy in my ear where she can talk to me.

ANNOUNCER 2. I want one.

ANNOUNCER 1. And so on behalf of Announcer 2, Beep and Bop – come on out guys! (**BEEP** *and* **BOP** *come on out.),* all of our fantastic Volunteers, the people deep deep in Beep's stomach and myself…wait… *(Finger to ear.)* Carol says you can have an ear thingy too!

ANNOUNCER 2. Yessss!

ANNOUNCER 1. And now I'll throw it over to Beep and Bop for a final word.

> *(Lights fade as everyone clears the stage. Spotlight on* **BEEP** *and* **BOP***.)*

BEEP. I don't know why…but I feel good, Bop.

BOP. Me too, Beep. Me too. Do you wanna sing a song?

BEEP. Nah. I just wanna stand here and…*be.*

BOP. Be. *(A longish beat.)* A lot of words start with the letter "B." Like…

BEEP. Beep.

BOP. Bop.

BEEP. Broom.

BOP. Blue.

BEEP. Berries.

BOP. Blueberries.

BEEP. Books.

BOP. Baboon.

BEEP. Balloon.

BOP. Bananas.

BEEP. Buttons.

BOP. Bunions.

BEEP. Barbecue.

BOP. Bumblebees.

BEEP. Backflip.

BOP. Butter.

BEEP. Bumpy.

BOP. Bermuda.

BEEP. Brontosaurus.

BOP. Bowl.

BEEP. Bankruptcy.

BOP. Ballistophobia.

BEEP. Bardolatry.

BOP. Barleycorn.

BEEP. Believe.

BOP. Buffalo.

BEEP. Baseball.

BOP. Brave.

BEEP. Best buds.

BOP. Bye.

BEEP. Bye.

(Blackout.)

End of Play

30 MILLION

Max Vernon & Jason Kim

30 MILLION was first presented by Keen Company (Jonathan Silverstein, Artistic Director; Mark Armstrong, Director of New Work) and Samuel French, Inc. as part of the 2016 Keen Teens Festival of New Work from May 13-15. The performance was directed by Mark Armstrong. The cast was as follows:

DEE DEE . . . . Melody Munitz

GORDON . . . . Brendan Manna

KEV . . . . Rose Hornyak

DENA . . . . Sherlicia Patrick

AUSTIN . . . . Edison Ventura Diaz

TOMMY . . . . Daniel Ramirez

FRANKIE . . . . Devante Rowe

TRACY . . . . Romy Bavli

RAY . . . . Marissa Harris

DERRICK . . . . Darren Valdera

CHARACTERS

DEE DEE

GORDON

KEV

DENA

AUSTIN

TOMMY

FRANKIE

TRACY

RAY

DERRICK

*(**DEE DEE** faces the audience.)*

DEE DEE. This is a story of how I became the world's most famous YouTube celebrity. It starts with an instrument I don't really know how to play. *(A guitar appears.)* A final hair and makeup check. *(A mirror appears.)* A best-gay-for-life.

*(**GORDON** appears.)*

GORDON. Hi.

DEE DEE. And a song I don't know how to sing. Oh. And, of course, an iPhone.

*(**GORDON** is recording **DEE DEE**. A shift.)*

Yo yo yo. This is Dee Dee otherwise known as Dakota D to anyone and everyone and no one in particular coming atcha from The Lou comma M-O. Whaaaat.

[MUSIC NO. 01: "FUN FUN FUN"]

GOT A TEXT
THERE'S A PARTY
I WANNA GO
SO MANY PEOPLE
THERE THAT I KNOW

WHOA-A-OH
WHOA-A-OH

MY MOM SAYS I
CAN'T STAY OUT LATE
BUT I SNEAK OUT THE FRONT DOOR
ANYWAY

HEY-E-EY
HEY-E-EY

COCA-COLA AND WHISKEY
FEELIN KINDA TIPSY
DOES ANYONE WANNA KISS ME?
AND

DEE DEE & GROUP.

I JUST WANNA HAVE FUN FUN FUN
I JUST WANNA GET DUMB DUMB DUMB
I JUST WANNA BE YOUNG YOUNG YOUNG
AND DANCE DANCE DANCE

OH I JUST WANNA HAVE FUN FUN FUN
I JUST WANNA GET DUMB DUMB DUMB
I JUST WANNA BE YOUNG YOUNG YOUNG
AND DANCE DANCE DANCE

GROUP.

DANCE DANCE DANCE DANCE
D-DANCE DANCE DANCE
D-DANCE DANCE DANCE

DEE DEE.

BOYS LOOKIN' AT ME
THE WHOLE NIGHT
CAUSE MY HAIR'S ON FLEEK
AND MY DRESS IS TIGHT

DEE DEE & GROUP.

AI-AI-AIGHT
AI-AI-AIGHT

DEE DEE.

THEY ALL WANNA KISS ME
THEY'RE LIKE

DEE DEE & MEN.

PLEASE

DEE DEE.

BUT I'M LIKE NO
CAUSE I'M A TEASE

DEE DEE & GROUP.

E-E EASE
E-E EASE

DEE DEE.

> VODKA AND SPRITE
> GOT ME FEELIN ALL RIGHT
> I'M GOIN' HARD TONIGHT
> AND

DEE DEE & GROUP.

> I JUST WANNA HAVE FUN FUN FUN
> I JUST WANNA GET DUMB DUMB DUMB
> I JUST WANNA BE YOUNG YOUNG YOUNG
> AND DANCE DANCE DANCE
>
> OH I JUST WANNA HAVE FUN FUN FUN
> I JUST WANNA GET DUMB DUMB DUMB
> I JUST WANNA BE YOUNG YOUNG YOUNG
> AND DANCE DANCE DANCE

GROUP.

> DANCE DANCE DANCE DANCE
> D-DANCE DANCE DANCE
> D-DANCE DANCE DANCE

DEE DEE.

> PUT YOUR HANDS IN THE AIR
> AND MAKE 'EM CLAP
> HECK YEAH, THAT'S RIGHT
> BOY I ALSO RAP
> EVERY DAY AT STARBUCKS
> I AM SIPPIN' A FRAP
> BUT I NEVER GET FAT
> 'CAUSE I GOT IT LIKE THAT
> BOYS AND GIRLS WANNA BE ME
> EVERYTIME THEY PARTY WITH DEE-DEE
> CAUSE I'M A WHOLE LOTTA FUN
> AND I'M HOT LIKE THE SUN
> AND I SPIT OUT HITS
> LIKE A MACHINE GUN

DEE DEE & GROUP.

> Y R U SO SERIOUS?
> D-D-D-DANCE TIL YOU'RE DELIRIOUS

DEE DEE.

> I JUST WANNA HAVE FUN FUN FUN
> I JUST WANNA GET DUMB DUMB DUMB
> I JUST WANNA BE YOUNG YOUNG YOUNG
> AND DANCE DANCE DANCE

> (**GROUP** *continues.*)

DEE DEE.

> I JUST WANNA HAVE FUN
> I JUST WANAN HAVE FUN

DEE DEE & GROUP.

> AND DANCE DANCE DANCE
> DANCE DANCE DANCE DANCE
> D-DANCE DANCE DANCE
> D-DANCE DANCE DANCE DANCE.

> (*A shift.*)

Do you think anyone will watch it?

GORDON. Hard to say. Depends how bored and sad they are I guess?

DEE DEE. Ugh. This is hopeless. We're only at – two hits. Two hits? Only two people / have watched it?!

GORDON. Well…we've watched it twice, so – I think it's just us.

DEE DEE. Nuh uh. We only watched it once. Definitely one other person in the universe has watched this and thought, "Oh my god, who is that really talented girl and how can I fulfill her lifelong dream of becoming the world's next Beyoncé with a dose of Ke$ha and Katy Perry and also, like, a splash of Lana Del Rey?"

GORDON. It started playing a second time while you were in the bathroom.

DEE DEE. You watched it again?

GORDON. No. It was on auto-play.

DEE DEE. Damn it!

GORDON. Do you think your mom's gonna get mad?

DEE DEE. Why would she get mad?

GORDON. I dunno, because. I mean, if she sees it, she's definitely not gonna like it.

DEE DEE. So?

GORDON. Did you ask her if –?

DEE DEE. I don't need to ask her. She doesn't get it. She just wants me to graduate already and start making money so she can stop working.

GORDON. I think you should ask her.

DEE DEE. Who cares. She's not gonna see it. She has a lot on her plate. It's hard to drink a bottle of wine every day.

GORDON. Wow – okay.

DEE DEE. You're right. Maybe we should take it down.

GORDON. You sure? I mean, up to you.

DEE DEE. Yeah. It was just for practice anyway. Let's take it down.

GORDON. Whoa.

DEE DEE. What?

GORDON. Dee Dee, look.

DEE DEE. Whaaaaat.

GORDON. Two hundred hits!

(*A shift.* **DENA** *and* **KEV.**)

DENA. Oh my god –

KEV. Oh wow –

DENA. Did you see –?

KEV. Watching now –

DENA. Crazy, right –

KEV. Holy sh–

DENA. See what I –

KEV. Maybe we should –

DENA. Really –?

KEV. Why not –?

DENA. I guess we could –

KEV. We can post so no one –

DENA. You mean, anonymous –?

KEV. Yeah –

DENA. Post it under –?

KEV. Yup –

DENA. Post it under Moderator –

KEV. That way –

DENA. No one knows who we are –

KEV. No one knows who we are –

DENA. Okay. Great idea.

> (**DENA** *and* **KEV** *are hidden.*)

Cool –

KEV. Cool –

DENA. Cool. But wait –

KEV. Yeah?

DENA. Are you sure we should –?

KEV. It's funny –

DENA. But we are –

KEV. It's funny –

DENA. But, like –

KEV. Not everything on the forum has to be about college admissions.

DENA. Alright. Done.

KEV. Oooh –

DENA. What? What –?

KEV. We already have a comment.

> (**AUSTIN**. *He's with* **TRACY**. **TOMMY** *and* **FRANKIE** *are also there.*)

AUSTIN. Hey hey hey. Come look at this.

TOMMY. Shit.

FRANKIE. Who is that?

AUSTIN. Wasn't she in geometry with us?

FRANKIE. Her face be fucked but her booty kinda swole. Kinda like you. You know, for a white girl you –

TRACY. Don't look at me, Frankie. *(Points to herself.)* This is not up for discussion.

AUSTIN. Yo, why you lookin' at my girlfriend?

FRANKIE. I'm just playin, man. Yo, don't get mad.

AUSTIN. Don't look at her.

FRANKIE. Alright cool.

AUSTIN. I said, look the other way.

FRANKIE. Aight. Word.

(**FRANKIE** *turns around.*)

AUSTIN. Alright, where was I? Right. Damn, this video —

TOMMY. I kinda like it —

AUSTIN. It's garbage.

TOMMY. Yeah. I hate it. I hate it. Where'd you find it?

AUSTIN. On the forum.

FRANKIE. Word. I had to get off the forum, man. Shit gets real on there.

AUSTIN. Didn't I tell you to look the other way?

FRANKIE. Yup. Thank you.

AUSTIN. What's wrong with him?

TRACY. I'm gonna post it on Facebook.

AUSTIN. Really?

TOMMY. Why?

TRACY. Because. She's stupid.

AUSTIN. What're you gonna say, baby?

(A shift.)

DEE DEE. "Fuck outta here with this messy ass ho. Bitch got beefy titties and no ass. Press play and luckfully you won't die like I did." Oh my god!

GORDON. Damnnn. She threw it down. What are you gonna do?

(A shift.)

DEE DEE. Excuse me. Tracy? Tracy Cox? Hi. It's me. Dee Dee? A-K-A Dakota D? We had geometry together last semester? I believe you posted my video with some, um, insulting words attached, and I was wondering if –

TRACY. Are you serious? I'm trying to eat my lunch.

DEE DEE. Right, but like, this is a democratic republic and I think we should be able to have conversations, lunch or no lunch, so –

TRACY. You're dumber than you look, huh?

DEE DEE. I'm actually kind of smart. But anyway. Can you please take it down? I didn't intend for it to be, like, *used* in this way.

TRACY. If you didn't want people to watch it, you shouldn't have posted it.

DEE DEE. Actually, I didn't. It was my friend Gordon, so if you could take it down now, or, if you don't possess a smartphone, then by tonight after you get home, I would really appreciate it.

TRACY. *(Beat.)* You know what I'm gonna do for you, Dee Dee?

DEE DEE. What?

TRACY. I'm gonna send it to my sister.

DEE DEE. Okay. Cool. But, um, who's your sister? And why would you do that?

TRACY. This conversation is over. You can go now.

DEE DEE. Um. But are you gonna – ?

AUSTIN. You heard him. It's over.

TOMMY. Yeah. It's over.

FRANKIE. See ya. Bye.

GORDON. Come on. Let's go.

> (**DEE DEE** *and* **GORDON** *leave.* **RAY** *and* **DERRICK.**)

RAY. Dude. They're such assholes.

DERRICK. They don't get it.

RAY. Get what?

DERRICK. It's not real.

RAY. What's not real?

DERRICK. Everything, man. This table. This fish stick. The ketchup. Her video.

RAY. What?

DERRICK. It's performance. It's all performance.

RAY. Totally. Uh huh. That's so smart. I know it seems like I'm the smart one, but you're so smart. *(Beat.)* Who do you think her sister is?

 (A shift.)

GORDON. *(Overlap with* **RAY***'s line.)* Who do you think her sister is?

DEE DEE. I don't know. But I don't have a good feeling about it.

GORDON. Me neither. Hey, FYI, America is a democracy. Not a democratic republic. We're not, like, ancient Rome. *(Beat.)* Just saying.

 (A shift.)

KEV AND DENA. "Seven Reasons Why the Youth of America Is In Trouble" by Tamara Cox writing for Buzzfeed.

TRACY. Seven. When asked what the First Amendment of the Constitution is, over twenty percent of high school students responded, "What?"

AUSTIN. Six. The American youth leads the world in eating disorders, childhood obesity, and venereal diseases, particularly herpes, crabs, and gonorrhea.

TOMMY. Five. The average American male will spend over ten thousand hours playing video games before the age of eighteen. That equals a little over four hundred and sixteen days.

FRANKIE. Four. We also spend over three hours per week watching pornography and under ten minutes per week reading for pleasure.

DERRICK. Three. Over twenty-five percent of teenagers report to binge drinking on a regular basis. Binge drinking is when you drink like your uncle at Thanksgiving and throw up after.

RAY. Two. Over forty percent of sexually active American teens have never come into contact with a condom.

TRACY. One. But the worst… Our entitlement. Take a look at this: a video posted by Missouri high schooler Dee Dee Lee, proclaiming herself the "next generation's everything."

> *(A shift.)*

DEE DEE. Gordon, what do we do? Do we hire an injunction? Can you buy an injunction?

GORDON. Do you know what an injunction is?

DEE DEE. Not really. But it's good, right?

GORDON. I think we should write to Tamara and ask her to take it down.

DEE DEE. She's not gonna listen.

GORDON. Why not?

DEE DEE. Because she is related to bitch on wheels Tracy Cox.

GORDON. Don't you think it's worth trying?

DEE DEE. She is not going to respond to an email.

GORDON. Maybe we should call her then.

DEE DEE. Do you think we can call the website and ask them to take it down?

GORDON. How do you *call* a website, / like what does that even mean?

DEE DEE. I don't know! At least I'm trying to use my brain!

GORDON. No, you're not. You barely have one.

DEE DEE. What is *that* supposed to mean? You better be careful, Gordon. Do you really want to piss off your *only* friend?

GORDON. Sometimes I don't even know why I'm friends with you.

DEE DEE. It's because I don't have any friends either. Can you please help me figure this out? Please?

> *(**DEE DEE**'s phone rings.)*

GORDON. Who is it?

DEE DEE. *(Phone.)* Hello? Yeah. This is Dee Dee. Uh huh… Uh huh… Uh huh… Okay… Okay, thank you.

GORDON. What? What? Are you okay? Dee Dee, what happened?

(A shift.)

DENA. I can't believe it.

KEV. I know.

DENA. Ellen?

KEV. I know.

DENA. She's gonna be on Ellen?!

KEV. Yeah.

DENA. Wait wait wait. Here she comes.

(Split.)

RAY. Here we go. Here we go!

(Split.)

FRANKIE. Let's get this party started, yo.

(They watch for several beats.)

RAY. Whoa.

AUSTIN. What's happening?

DENA. Jesus.

FRANKIE. Yo, what's she doing?

RAY. She just skipped a whole verse –

TRACY. Ha!

KEV. Look at her –

DENA. She's freaking out –

TOMMY. Is she crying?

RAY. Oh no! I think she's crying!

FRANKIE. Yo.

TOMMY. Holy shit.

FRANKIE. That's bad. That's bad.

TRACY. Where the fuck is she –?

RAY. She's running off the stage!

DENA. Damn.

KEV. Ouch.

TOMMY. Wow.

RAY. Man…

DENA. Oh my god.

KEV. Wait. They're following her. They're following her!

TOMMY. Shit, look at her crying in her dressing room.

FRANKIE. Damn, yo. She's sobbing.

DERRICK. I bet she's doing it on purpose.

RAY. What do you mean?

DERRICK. It's art. It's a part of her art.

AUSTIN. Babe, are you getting this?

TRACY. Nope.

RAY. I can't watch. / I can't watch anymore.

AUSTIN. How come? You should record it.

RAY. Turn it off. Hey, come on.

TRACY. I don't need to.

RAY. Come on, turn it off.

AUSTIN. Why not?

TRACY. It's gonna be everywhere the minute it's over.

RAY. Turn it off! Turn it off! Turn it off!

(Beat.)

DERRICK. Damn, man.

RAY. Sorry. I'm sorry. It's just… She's crying. On national TV.

(A shift.)

DEE DEE. Hey. So. Thank you for watching my performance last week. I know that it wasn't perfect. But nothing in the world is. Including me. I'm not ashamed I made some mistakes. I'm actually determined to do better. A lot of you have been messaging me on social media asking when my album is gonna come out. And, I can't say too much at the moment, but I promise you are in for a treat. Soon. In the meantime, here's a song I wrote. It's for all the haters out there.

[MUSIC NO. 02: "YOU DON'T KNOW ME"]

I HAVE TWO EARS
THEY HEARD WHAT YOU CALLED
ME BEHIND MY BACK
THAT WAS WHACK
I HAVE NO FEARS
YOU KICKED ME IN THE FACE
BUT I'LL KICK YOU BACK
SNEAK ATTACK!

GOT A BROKEN HEART, BROKEN HOME
BROKE THE INTERNET BUT STILL I'M ALONE
WHILE STRANGERS WATCH ME ON THEIR SCREENS
BUT YOU DON'T KNOW ME! YOU'LL NEVER KNOW ME!
MY FAKE ASS FRIENDS ARE ALL TELLING LIES
BUT I'M A PUZZLE, A VERY HARD PUZZLE
SO MANY PIECES, ALL DIFFERENT SIZE
AND I CAN'T HEAR A WORD YOU SAY

BULLIES.

BET YOU SUCK A HUNDRED DICKS A DAY.

DEE DEE.

ALL YOU HATERS GO AWAYYYYYY
CAUSE YOU DON'T KNOW ME. YOU'LL NEVER KNOW ME!

DON'T BE JEALOUS
IT'S NOT MY FAULT THAT I'M COOLER
THAN AN ESKIMO IN THE SNOW.

I'M NOT RICH, JUST FAMOUS
IT WAS FUN AT FIRST, BUT NOW IT KINDA BLOWS

DEE DEE & BULLIES.

UH OH

DEE DEE.

FIRST YOU'RE NO ONE
THEN A CELEBRITY
THIRTY MILLION PEOPLE WANNA SEE
AND YOU CAN'T TELL WHO YOU'D RATHER BE

DEE DEE & BULLIES.

> BUT YOU DON'T KNOW ME! YOU'LL NEVER KNOW ME!
> MY FAKE ASS FRIENDS

DEE DEE.

> ARE ALL TELLING LIES
> BUT I'M A PUZZLE, A VERY HARD PUZZLE
> SO MANY PIECES, ALL DIFFERENT SIZE
> AND I CAN'T HEAR A WORD YOU SAY

BULLIES.

> YOU'RE A DUMB ASS BITCH AND YOU'RE PROBABLY GAY

DEE DEE.

> ALL YOU HATERS GO AWAYYYYYY
> CAUSE YOU DON'T KNOW ME. YOU'LL NEVER KNOW!
> I'M THE BIGGEST THING IN MY WHOLE TOWN

BULLIES.

> YOU'RE RETARDED. LAUGH OUT LOUD!

DEE DEE.

> SO WHY DOES IT FEEL LIKE I'M DROWNING?
> YOU DON'T KNOW ME! YOU'LL NEVER KNOW ME!
> SO MANY PEOPLE ARE ALL TELLING LIES
> BUT I'M A PUZZLE, A VERY HARD PUZZLE
> SO MANY PIECES…
> BUT YOU DON'T KNOW ME! YOU'LL NEVER KNOW ME!

DEE DEE & BULLIES.

> MY FAKE ASS FRIENDS ARE ALL TELLING LIES
> BUT I'M A PUZZLE, A VERY HARD PUZZLE
> SO MANY PIECES,

DEE DEE.

> ALL DIFFERENT SIZE
> AND I DON'T HEAR A WORD YOU SAY

EVERYONE ELSE.

> STOP SINGIN' AND KILL YOURSELF TODAY.

DEE DEE.

> ALL YOU HATERS GO AWAYYYYYY
> CAUSE YOU DON'T KNOW ME. YOU'LL NEVER KNOW ME!
>> *(A shift.)*

GORDON. You okay?

DEE DEE. Yeah. Why wouldn't I be?

GORDON. Well, cause. Are you sure?

DEE DEE. I'm fine.

GORDON. Did someone actually get in touch with you about recording an album, or –?

DEE DEE. No. But someone will. Any minute now.

GORDON. Hey, Dee Dee, do you maybe want to –

DEE DEE. What?

GORDON. We don't have to post any more if you don't want to.

DEE DEE. What are you talking about?

GORDON. I just mean, you don't have to keep doing this if you don't want to.

DEE DEE. Gordon, this is what I've always wanted.

GORDON. Okay. Want me to post this one?

DEE DEE. Yes.

(*A shift.*)

TRACY. I can't believe it. I can't believe it.

AUSTIN. The first one gets ten million in two weeks and this one gets thirty million views in two days?

TRACY. That's like, the population of a small country. No. No. / No. No. No.

AUSTIN. Baby. Baby, calm down.

TRACY. Don't call me baby. Not right now. She actually got a record deal. Columbia Records gave her a record deal!

AUSTIN. So?

TRACY. What do you mean, so?

AUSTIN. Who cares?

TRACY. I care.

AUSTIN. Why?

TRACY. Because. She's a dumb bitch. (*Beat.*) I'm gonna ruin her. Austin, you have to help me figure something out. I'm gonna ruin her sad sad little life. Austin? Are you listening?

AUSTIN. Yeah. Okay. / Whatever.

TRACY. Fucking bitch…

FRANKIE. Yo, let me ask you a question.

TRACY. I told you don't talk to me.

FRANKIE. You jealous?

TRACY. What?

FRANKIE. I said, are you jealous?

TRACY. What are you talking about? I'm not – no – what?! Fuck you, Frankie. Austin! Aren't you gonna say something?

AUSTIN. Yeah, fuck you, Frankie. Tommy, say something.

TOMMY. Fuck you, Frankie.

FRANKIE. Man, y'all are some dumb assholes, man.

AUSTIN. What're you talking about? You're the asshole.

TOMMY. Yeah. You're the asshole.

FRANKIE. Y'all don't even know what you're talking about. You, you think you cool just cause you got a girlfriend and shit. And you, you gay as a Christmas tree and you don't even know it. And you're just a mean ass do nothing but talk talk talk bitch. I don't need to be y'alls friend just cause we teammates. You ain't even a good quarterback. You can't throw for shit and you skinny as a motherfucker. Stop putting the black man down, man. I'm done with this. We done.

(FRANKIE *leaves.*)

TRACY. Whatever.

TOMMY. I fucked a chick last week in the back of my mom's mini-van.

TRACY. Shut up, Tommy. Austin, where you going?

AUSTIN. I'm going to apologize.

TRACY. What? Are you serious?

AUSTIN. Yo, we've been friends since we were, like, five.

TRACY. Austin! If you leave, I am going to break up with you. Do you hear me? I'm going to dump you so fast your face is gonna fall off.

AUSTIN. Alright. Cool.

(**AUSTIN** *leaves.*)

TOMMY. Do you want a tissue?

TRACY. Go away, Tommy.

(**TOMMY** *leaves. A shift. Everyone is hidden.*)

DENA. Did you guys hear?

KEV. Someone slashed Dee Dee's tires this morning.

RAY. Seriously?

DENA. And just yesterday, someone sprayed C-U-N-T on her locker.

RAY. Jesus.

KEV. I heard the football team egged her house. Three times.

DENA. I heard someone tried to attack her. In public.

RAY. Where?

KEV. Like, on the street.

DENA. Someone pushed her against a wall and spit gum in her hair and ran away before she could see who it was.

KEV. Her video is in the *Guinness Book of World Records* as the most disliked video of all time on the *entire* internet.

DENA. Someone took a picture of her crying in the bathroom the other day and now she's a meme.

RAY. What?

KEV. It's a picture of snot coming out of her nose and it says #sadpancakes on it.

DENA. Fran Lebowitz called her the "nadir of millenial culture."

KEV. Who's Fran Lebowitz?

DENA. No idea. I think she's a chef.

KEV. Did you hear someone leaked a video of Dee Dee's mom driving drunk and now she might go to jail?

DENA. Oh, and her record deal?

KEV. It fell apart.

DENA. They say it might've even been a prank.

KEV. I know, right?

DENA. Anyway, point is, I heard she didn't apply to any schools thinking she was gonna be famous and now she can't even go to college.

KEV. Tell us where you got in as your acceptance letters arrive. We heard Ray321 got into Harvard and Yale.

RAY. Yup.

DENA. Congrats.

KEV. Yay!

RAY. Thanks, guys. D-Day819 got into Vassar and Berkeley.

DENA. Whoa, really?

DERRICK. Yeah, really.

DENA. What did they write their essay about?

DERRICK. Art. Art and responsibility. Dee Dee posted a video. And she got slaughtered. But that's the price you pay for being an artist. That's the gift you get for the gift you put out into the world. What happened to Dee Dee, I don't feel bad for her. 'Cause that's on her. She knew what she was getting into. She deserves it.

RAY. Dude. No, she doesn't.

DERRICK. You're just saying that because you were also bullied growing up. You're projecting. That's Freud.

RAY. What are you talking about? I thought you were smart, but you're full of shit. I can't be friends with you.

DERRICK. Whatever. I don't need friends, man. The world is a dark place and we are all alone.

DENA. Okay, great. Well, I have gotten into Michigan State and also Mizzou.

KEV. See you guys soon. Signing off –

    (A shift.)

DEE DEE. Hey.

GORDON. Hey.

DEE DEE. So? Did you get in?

GORDON. Yeah.

DEE DEE. That's great, Gordon.

GORDON. Thanks.

DEE DEE. Your dream school.

GORDON. I know, right. Kinda cool.

DEE DEE. Don't forget our deal. You have to design my red carpet dresses. Even when you're famous.

GORDON. What do I get in return?

DEE DEE. Exposure. Duh.

GORDON. Deal.

DEE DEE. Deal.

GORDON. Hey, how's your mom?

DEE DEE. She promised the judge she'd go to rehab.

GORDON. That's good.

DEE DEE. And then she vomited at the bar and I had to go pick her up.

GORDON. Sorry.

DEE DEE. It's all right.

GORDON. Do you know what you're gonna do yet?

DEE DEE. I guess I'll just, I dunno, hang out for a year? Get my job back at Froyo Joe's and write some more songs?

GORDON. Are you sure you want to do that?

DEE DEE. It's not like there's a better job around town.

GORDON. No, I mean write more songs.

DEE DEE. What do you mean?

GORDON. Dee Dee… I know "Fun Fun Fun" was a big hit, but… Maybe you should… Have you ever thought about, I dunno, doing something more practical?

DEE DEE. You're starting to sound like my mom.

GORDON. I'm just saying, it might be useful if –

DEE DEE. What, you want me to go learn a skill? Like become an accountant? / A secretary?

GORDON. No, that's not what I meant, of course you can do more than that, it's just –

DEE DEE. I know the Columbia Records thing was a fluke, but there will be someone else. My job is to work hard at my music. And I will. And someone will come through. I know it.

GORDON. You can't even show your face at school anymore, Dee Dee. People throw things at you. Someone tried to burn your car.

DEE DEE. They're just jealous. I am an internet celebrity.

GORDON. Exactly. You are an *internet* celebrity. Do you know what happens to internet celebrities?

DEE DEE. Why are you being so mean?

GORDON. I'm trying to help you.

DEE DEE. You think I like being tortured? You think I enjoy it?

GORDON. No, of course you don't –

DEE DEE. You don't think I've stayed up thinking how my life would be different if you hadn't done this to me?

GORDON. What do you – what are you talking about?

DEE DEE. Last time I checked, this was *your* fault.

GORDON. What? How is it / my fault?

DEE DEE. It was your idea to record a video.

GORDON. No, it wasn't.

DEE DEE. Yes, it was. You said, "Why don't you record this? It's catchy!"

GORDON. Yeah, I mean, for your own archives. Not put it up all over the internet so people can watch it and laugh in your face.

DEE DEE. *You* posted it.

GORDON. You *told me* to post it.

DEE DEE. I was high.

GORDON. No, you weren't.

DEE DEE. I meant high in the general sense, like, high off the energy of my performance, not high / on drugs high –

GORDON. Dee Dee, it's *your* video. It's yours.

DEE DEE. You taped me! This is abuse!

GORDON. Dee Dee, are you out of your mind? You *asked* me to tape you!

DEE DEE. You're such a fucking wimp.

GORDON. No, I'm not! How am I a wimp?

DEE DEE. You are. You are a soggy, wet, teeny little wimp. / You're seaweed.

GORDON. Look, just because you have *zero* talent, and now you're being made an example of, as you probably should, doesn't mean you get to act like a complete asshole.

DEE DEE. Excuse me?

GORDON. Dee Dee, you can't sing.

DEE DEE. I have a perfectly average to above average voice.

GORDON. Exactly.

DEE DEE. Have you heard of Britney Spears?

GORDON. Britney Spears is pretty.

DEE DEE. Well, it's no wonder your parents put you up for adoption. You are a spineless nothing. No one's ever gonna love you. Ever. *(Beat.)* Wait. Gordon. No. I didn't mean that. No –

(**GORDON** *is gone.*)

Shit.

(A shift.)

TRACY. What's your name again?

GORDON. Gordon.

TRACY. Right. Gordon. You sure you want to do this?

GORDON. Absolutely.

TRACY. Wow. She must've said something really nasty. What'd she say?

GORDON. None of your business.

TRACY. You're lucky I agreed to do this.

GORDON. You approached me. It was your idea.

TRACY. I knew something was up when you two stopped sitting at lunch together. I had a feeling.

GORDON. How come none of your boys are here?

TRACY. I'm a solo act now. Whatever. It's better this way. I'm way too pretty for everyone at this school anyway. Did you hear she got another record deal?

GORDON. Yeah.

TRACY. Is it true?

GORDON. I don't know.

TRACY. I bet you it is. Fucking bitch. I bet you she got signed by Jay-Z's label or something and drops a surprise album and becomes best friends with Taylor Swift and they go to Paris together and ride around in jet skis. Fuck.

GORDON. Or she could flame out in a month, get that "Oh, I feel like I've seen you in something" squint everywhere she goes for the rest of her life, feel bad about herself forever. No one is taking her seriously anyway.

TRACY. Hey, can I ask you a question? You posted that video on purpose, right?

GORDON. What do you mean?

TRACY. Like, to spite her?

GORDON. No. We were having fun. We thought it was good.

TRACY. Yeah… At first I thought, maybe I actually kinda liked it? But I was wrong.

(DEE DEE *enters.*)

GORDON. Hey. Dee Dee.

DEE DEE. What, you're talking to me now? Sorry, I really can't be seen over here at the – how do I put this politely – loser table – but I just wanted to let you know, Tracy, that my new label is suing your sister for libel. They're going to keep suing her until you and your whole family and all their kids have to live on the street and then they're going to sue everyone again until all of you jump off a bridge. And Gordon, it's great to see that you have another friend now. Maybe people won't think you're so pathetic anymore.

TRACY. Now!

> (**TRACY** *grabs* **DEE DEE**, *rips her shirt open.* **GORDON** *snaps a pic.*)

DEE DEE. What the fuck! I'm not wearing a bra!

TRACY. Did you get that?

GORDON. Yup.

DEE DEE. What are you gonna do with that? Guys. Guys? Gordon? Why are you doing this to me? What did I ever do to you?

TRACY. You exist. That's what you did to me.

> (**DEE DEE** *cries.*)

Oh my god. Are you crying?

DEE DEE. I'm asking you, as a human being. Delete the picture. Please.

> (*Beat.*)

TRACY. No. Every time anyone searches for your name, it's gonna be there. You, naked.

> (*Beat.*)

DEE DEE. Fine. What do I care. Everyone thinks I'm a joke anyway. Go ahead. Post it. It'll probably raise my profile. (**DEE DEE** *turns around to go.*) Gordon, I… Please… Please, Gordon.

> (**DEE DEE** *exits.*)

TRACY. I wanted to be a singer when I was little. My parents told me I wasn't talented enough.

GORDON. That sucks. (*Beat.*) At least you had parents.

TRACY. Yeah… I guess… Do you think I should still try to go to vet school?

GORDON. I don't really care.

TRACY. Yeah… Me neither… Hey, what are you doing? What the fuck is your problem! Why did you delete that? What's wrong with you?

(A shift.)

DEE DEE. Hey guys. I wrote something new. And, yeah. Who knows what will happen with it. If there is one thing I've realized, it's that there is no such thing as certainty in life. A lot of you have been asking if the rumors are true. And I'm sad to report that yes, I will no longer be putting out a record with Sony. But, I do have some new material I want to share. With you. Directly. From me to you. From my heart to your ears. Alright. Here we go.

[MUSIC NO. 03: "PLEASE SUBSCRIBE"]

THERE'S THINGS THAT I DON'T UNDERSTAND
LIKE HOW TO LIVE IN INFAMY
MY WHOLE LIFE IS MYSTERY
'CAUSE EVERYTHING THAT I PLANNED
KEEPS TURNING OUT SO DIFFERENTLY
TELL ME WHAT'S MY DESTINY?

I HOPE HATE DON'T LAST FOREVER
I HEAR EVERY WORD YOU SAY
CAN I CLOSE MY EYES AND FADE AWAY?

CAN I TAKE IT BACK?
BACK TO BEFORE
WHEN I WAS JUST A TEENAGE GIRL
WITH A GUITAR AND NOTHING MORE
BEFORE THE HATE, AND ALL THE LIES
I WASN'T COOL, HAD ONE FRIEND AT SCHOOL,
AND THIS DREAM I HAD TO TRY.

AND I DON'T KNOW WHERE I'M GOING NOW.

THERE'S THINGS THAT I DID NOT EXPECT
MY FACE ON THIRTY MILLION SCREENS,
RECORD DEALS AND P.R. TEAMS
AND A LIFETIME OF REGRET
I LOST MYSELF, I LOST A FRIEND,
TELL ME WHEN THE NIGHTMARE ENDS

I

DEE DEE & SOLO VOICE.

HOPE HATE DON'T LAST FOREVER

DEE DEE.

I

DEE DEE & SOLO VOICE.

HEAR EVERY WORD YOU SAY
TRY TO CLOSE MY EYES AND FADE AWAY

DEE DEE.

CAN I TAKE IT BACK
BACK TO BEFORE

(**ENSEMBLE** *"Ooh's" underneath.*)

WHEN I WAS JUST A TEENAGE GIRL
WITH A GUITAR AND NOTHING MORE
BEFORE THE HATE, AND ALL THE LIES
I WASN'T COOL, HAD ONE FRIEND AT SCHOOL,
AND THIS DREAM I HAD TO TRY.

(**ENSEMBLE** *stops "Ooh's".*)

AND I DON'T KNOW WHERE I'M GOING NOW.

YOU BUILT ME UP, YOU MADE ME FALL
YOU PUSHED ME DOWN BUT I WON'T CRAWL
'CAUSE I'M STILL STRONG AND I'LL STAND TALL

ENSEMBLE.

TALL
TALL
TALL
TALL

DEE DEE & ENSEMBLE.

CAN I TAKE IT BACK
BACK TO BEFORE
WHEN I WAS JUST A TEENAGE GIRL
WITH A GUITAR AND NOTHING MORE
BEFORE THE HATE, AND ALL THE LIES
I WASN'T COOL, HAD ONE FRIEND AT SCHOOL,
AND THIS DREAM I HAD TO TRY.

AND I DON'T KNOW WHERE I'M GOING NOW

NO I DON'T KNOW WHERE I'M GOING NOW
SAID I DON'T KNOW WHERE I'M GOING NOW
DEE DEE.
PLEASE SUBSCRIBE.

End of Musical